THE WAR OF THE WORLDS

THE WAR OF THE WORLDS

By H. G. Wells

Adapted by Mary Ann Evans

Illustrated by Paul Wenzel

Step into Classics™

Random House 🏠 New York

http://www.randomhouse.com/

Library of Congress Cataloging-in-Publication Data
Evans, Mary Ann.
The war of the worlds / H. G. Wells ; adapted by Mary Ann Evans;
illustrated by Paul Wenzel.
    p.   cm. — (Step into classics)
SUMMARY: As life on Mars becomes impossible, Martians and their
terrifying machines invade the earth.
ISBN 0-679-81047-1 (pbk.) — ISBN 0-679-91047-6 (lib. bdg.)
[1. Science fiction.]   I. Wenzel, Paul (Paul Edward), ill.
II. Wells, H. G. (Herbert George), 1866–1946. War of the worlds.
III. Title.   IV. Series: Step into Classics.
PZ7.E89195War   1991   [Fic]—dc20   90-52936
Printed in the United States of America   10 9

Chapter 1

No one even dreamed that the planet Earth was being watched. No one even gave much thought to life on other planets. A few scientists, at most, imagined that there might be some sort of life on Mars. Some sort of plants or maybe animals. But no one thought of danger.

People went about their work and their play. They were sure that humans were more intelligent than any other living thing.

But those who watched us were more intelligent than we are. More intelligent than we could even imagine. And need had brightened their minds and made them sharp. Need had hardened their hearts.

Mars is much older than Earth, and much smaller. It is also much farther from the sun. Mars has become very cold in its old age. Its seas have shrunk, and its icecaps have grown. Soon life there will become impossible.

The Martians must have watched Earth through telescopes. They saw green hills and blue water. And they felt hope. Warm Earth was a place they could live. They carefully planned their move.

The Martians think of people on Earth as we think of monkeys. Or even ants. Human life means very little to them. Killing us so that they could live would not matter.

But don't judge them too quickly. We humans have killed off many animals with no thought. The bison is gone. So is the dodo. When Europeans moved to new lands, they swept away the people living there. So who are we to judge the Martians?

Our problem with the Martians started six years ago, on August 12, 1902. An astronomer, a scientist who studies stars, was watching Mars. At midnight he saw a huge ball of fire shooting toward Earth very fast. It disappeared in fifteen minutes.

There was almost nothing in the newspapers about it the next day. Just a few lines on a back page. Only a few scientists knew about the strange ball of fire.

My friend Ogilvy was a well-known astronomer. And he was excited! The next night he asked me to watch Mars with him.

I looked through Ogilvy's telescope. Mars looked so small in the blackness. After all, it is forty million miles away. Forty million miles of empty space.

That night we saw another ball of fire leave Mars. A reddish flash appeared just as the clock struck midnight. We watched the fireball travel toward Earth.

We had no idea then that these two balls of fire were spaceships. I thought that Mars was trying to signal us.

Ogilvy laughed. "There's one chance in a million that there's anything with a brain on Mars!"

He thought that we were seeing meteorites. That's the name astronomers give to falling stars. He thought that a shower of meteorites was hitting Mars. Or maybe a volcano was exploding.

But that was not the end of the strange balls of fire. Each night at midnight another flash was seen. Night after night for ten nights.

The newspapers picked up the news at last. But still no one was worried. Life went on as always.

Then came the night of the first "falling star." That's what we thought it was. Hundreds must have seen it. A line of fire high in the sky rushing to the east. People thought it was just another meteorite. But it wasn't.

That night no one looked for the meteorite. But Ogilvy went to look for it very early the next morning. He was sure it had fallen near Woking, our town.

And find it he did, in a field outside of Woking. The force of its landing had made a very large hole in the ground. Some nearby grass was on fire.

The Thing itself was almost all buried in sand. Only the top stuck out. It looked like a huge tin can. It was about ninety feet across.

Ogilvy was surprised at its size and shape. Most fallen stars are round. But this was a cylinder. A giant can that seemed designed by someone.

Ogilvy wanted to go right up to it. But the Thing was still too hot from its flight. He could not get near it.

A strange, hissing noise was coming from inside. But strangest of all to my friend was what he saw next. The top of the "can" was turning. This was no meteorite!

It took Ogilvy a few minutes to understand. Something was inside the

Thing! And that something was turning the top to open it.

"Good heavens!" said Ogilvy. "There are men in there. They must be half roasted to death! They're trying to get out!"

Then he thought of the flashing balls of fire on Mars. He guessed that the Thing came from Mars. The cylinder must be a spaceship!

Ogilvy wanted to help the men inside get out. But it was still too hot to get near.

He ran wildly toward the town. He begged for help. People thought he was a madman. No one stopped when he called to them.

Then he saw someone he knew. Henderson, the reporter. Ogilvy told Henderson what he had seen. The two men ran back out to the Thing.

It was cooler now. Air was either coming in or going out of the rim. It made a thin sizzling sound. They tapped the side of the Thing with a stick. No one answered.

"I think they must be dead," Henderson said.

Ogilvy agreed. So the two men went back to town. Henderson sent the strange story to his newspaper in London.

Meanwhile, word of the amazing Thing spread through the town of Woking. Some people marched right out to the Thing. They wanted to see the "dead men from Mars." So did I.

Chapter 2

By evening there must have been a few hundred people around the pit. Some had come from far away to see the Thing from Mars. There were piles of bicycles and a fancy carriage. The crowd was excited.

I passed a boy running.

"It's moving!" he said to me. "The top keeps turning. I don't like it. I'm going home."

The boy surprised me. I could hardly wait to see what was in the Thing.

I pushed my way through the crowd. I saw a man climb out of the pit. The crowd had pushed him in.

Ogilvy called to me. He and Henderson were in the pit. They were digging the Thing out.

"Help keep the crowd back," Ogilvy said. "We don't know what's inside the cylinder!"

But I had no time to do anything. Just then the top of the huge Thing came off. It fell into the sand.

I think everyone watched for something like a human to come out. I know I did. Instead I saw two bright disks. Like eyes. Then out of the shadows came what looked like a little gray snake. Then another. And another. These were tentacles. But I could not see the creature they were attached to.

A sudden chill came over me. Someone screamed. People could not take their eyes off what they were

seeing. More and more long tentacles appeared. The people all moved back. Horror took the place of surprise on their faces.

Soon everyone ran off. I was alone. Too scared to move.

A big gray round thing rose out of the cylinder. Slowly. Painfully. It looked like a great big head. No body. Just a head.

Two big dark eyes looked at me. Under them was a mouth without lips. Shaped like a V. It shook and panted and dropped spit.

The Martian monster had no chin. What it did have were tentacles. Lots of them. Its skin was very oily. Its breathing was very loud. The air on Earth and the pull of gravity were different than on Mars. Breathing and moving were difficult for the Martian.

I felt sick with disgust and fear as I watched.

Suddenly the Martian fell over with a loud thud. "Ulla!" howled the monster. It disappeared into the hole.

Then another Martian came out of the cylinder. At that, I ran in a mad panic. I stopped at the first group of trees I saw. I stood panting. Other people were standing around like me. We all stared in horror at the pit. Scared but unable to stop looking.

For a second, a leash of thin black whips flashed over the pit. Like the arms of an octopus. Then a thin rod rose up. On its top was a flat metal disk. It spun around. What could be going on there?

The sun was going down. But other people still stood there as I did. Frozen with fear and fascination. We could not stop looking.

"What ugly beasts!" said a neighbor of mine. "What ugly beasts," he said again and again.

Hardly anything was moving in the pit. The people began to feel braver. Slowly they moved closer to the hole. A few walked boldly into it.

Ogilvy and Henderson went right

up to the pit. They waved a white flag. A white flag means "peace" to us. The men were trying to tell the Martians that we meant them no harm.

All at once, there was a flash of light. Three green smoky puffs came out of the pit. They were very bright—almost like flames. At the same time, I could hear a hissing sound. Soon the hissing became a loud hum.

Slowly a large shape rose out of the pit. A beam of hot light came out of it. The beam hit Ogilvy and Henderson and the white flag. It set them on fire. The crowd turned and ran in terror.

I stood staring. The beam moved. Everyone and everything in its path flashed into white flame and fell. The trees and nearby houses burst into flames. Soon there was fire all around. The Martians' light beam melted glass and metal. Everything.

All this took place so quickly that I was stunned. I could not move to run away. By a stroke of luck I had escaped the beam. I saw the heat-ray machine sink back into the pit. I was still alive. Alone and without protection in the dark.

But suddenly fear hit me. I turned and ran in a panic. I did not dare to look back. I was crying like a child.

Chapter 3

I kept on running until I could run no more. I fell and lay still at the side of the road.

When I awoke, I was confused. How did I get there? Where was my hat? My collar? Then I remembered. The pit. The Thing with its deadly beam. My terror.

I started to walk, but I felt weak. I walked like a drunk man.

Life around me seemed normal. I passed workmen. Women with baskets. Children. A train rushed by. I was amazed. I had just come from such horror. And now it was gone. How could that be?

I stopped to talk to a group of people.

"What's the news?" I asked.

"People seem all silly about something," said a woman. "What's it all about?"

"Haven't you heard of the monsters from Mars?" said I.

"Quite enough, thanks," she said.

All the people laughed.

I felt foolish and angry. I tried to tell them what I had seen. But I could not get the words out. They laughed again.

"You will hear more yet," I said. I shook my head sadly and went home.

My wife was shocked by how I looked. And scared by what I told her. Her face was white with fear.

"They may come here," she kept saying.

"They are very slow," I said. "They may kill those who come near them. But they are too weak to get out of the pit."

Saying this cheered me more than my wife. She was still worried.

"On Earth, gravity is three times as strong as on Mars," I explained. "Poor Ogilvy told me so. The Martians weigh three times as much on Earth as they do on Mars. They can hardly move. They can't hurt us. Don't worry."

The newspapers said the same.

But we did not think of two other facts. Earth has much more oxygen than Mars. The extra oxygen would make up for the stronger pull of gravity. And the Martians had machines to do their work. Machines that could move very well.

Chapter 4

The Martians came out of the cylinder on a Friday evening. That night, most people acted as if Mars were not even in the sky. They worked, ate, and went to bed. Trains stopped and went on as always.

Only near the pit were things strange. A few houses were still burning. The people in nearby houses kept lights on all night. They did not sleep.

Hammering came from the pit all night long. And now and then a puff of green smoke rose into the sky. The cylinder was like a poisoned dart, stuck into the Earth. But the poison was just beginning to work.

At about eleven o'clock soldiers started arriving in Woking. The military knew the situation was serious.

At midnight some people saw a green star fall. The second cylinder.

On Saturday I got up early. I had not slept well. The milkman came as always. He said that soldiers now circled the pit.

"The soldiers have orders. They may not destroy the Martians," he said. "Not unless the Martians attack first."

The man next-door was in his garden. He gave me some berries.

"Another one of those spaceship things fell last night," he said. "The pine woods around it are still on fire. One cylinder would have been enough. Those Martians will cost a lot of money!" he said, laughing. But then he grew serious. "Poor Ogilvy."

After breakfast I walked toward the pit. I saw some soldiers on the way and talked with them.

None of them had seen the Martians. So I described the heat-ray to them.

They began to argue about how to fight the Martians.

"Crawl up to them under cover," said one. "Then rush them."

"No," said another. "You can't hide from this heat-ray thing. It will cook you. You have to dig a hole to be safe."

"You and your holes!" said a third. "You sound like a rabbit."

Another soldier asked me to describe the Martians. I did.

"Octopuses," said he. "That is what they are. We are fighting against fish this time."

They talked on as I left them. But I could not get near the pit that day. Soldiers were all around. So I went home and took a cool bath. The day was very hot.

The newspaper said the Martians stayed in the pit all day. They kept hammering. They were getting ready for a fight.

Another man had tried to signal them. He had a flag on a long pole. The Martians ignored it. Just as we would ignore the moo of a cow.

At about three o'clock I heard the thud of a gunshot. And then more thuds. Soldiers were shooting at the second cylinder. They hoped to destroy it before it opened. At last a big field cannon arrived. The soldiers were sure it would do the job.

My wife and I were having tea. We heard a blast that came from near the pit.

Then we heard a great crash very close to us. It shook the ground. The college next door was tumbling down. The treetops burst into flame. One of our chimneys cracked. Broken pieces of it fell into our flower bed.

My wife and I stood amazed. Then it came to me. The college no longer blocked our house. The heat-ray could hit us now!

I grabbed my wife's arm.

"We can't stay here," I said.

"But where are we to go?" asked my wife. And then she answered her own question.

"To my cousins in Leatherhead!"

I looked down the hill. People were coming out of their houses, scared. Soon they would all be leaving Woking. Most of them would take the other road. I was sure the road to Leatherhead would be less crowded.

"Stay here," I said to my wife. "You are safe for a time."

I rushed to the Spotted Dog Inn. The landlord had a horse and cart. I rented it for two times what he asked. I said I would have it back by midnight.

"What's going on?" he asked.

I told him that I had to leave my house. And that was true.

My wife watched the horse and cart. I ran into our house. I threw our silver and a few other things into a tablecloth. The trees below the house were burning. I worked as fast as I could.

Just then a soldier came running up. He was going from house to

house. He was warning people to get out fast.

My wife and I were soon on our way. The road ahead looked clear and peaceful. Behind us was red fire and thick black smoke. The road was dotted with people running.

"The Martians must be setting fire to everything their heat-ray can reach," I said.

I made sure the horse moved very fast.

Chapter 5

The heavy firing of guns stopped suddenly. The road was peaceful. We got to Leatherhead by nine o'clock. The trip went well. The horse had a rest. I had dinner with cousins and a silent wife.

Then I left for home. The horse and cart had to be back by midnight. I would keep my promise.

As I got near Woking I could see a red glow. Driving storm clouds mixed with black and red smoke.

All at once I saw a green light falling through the sky. It landed in a nearby field. It was the third falling star! More Martians!

But then the storm began. Lightning flashed. Thunder burst around my ears. Soaking wet, I drove on as fast as I could.

And then I saw a new monster. How can I describe it? Huge. Taller than many houses. It walked with big steps on three long legs. Smashing trees with each step. Its metal body clattered as it walked. Steel ropes swung from its sides. The clatter mixed with the sound of thunder.

Then suddenly a second metal monster appeared. It looked just like the first. It was rushing toward me!

I tried to turn out of the way. I pulled the horse's head hard to the right. Too hard. The cart turned over. It fell upon the horse. I was thrown into a pool of water.

I crawled right out and hid in some bushes. The horse lay still. Poor thing. It was dead.

In another moment, the monster walked right by me. It kept going. Then it was gone. But I could hear it calling to the first monster, "Aloo! Aloo!"

I was soaking wet. I needed to find someplace dry and safe.

I saw a small hut. I banged and banged at the locked door. But there was no answer. So I crawled into the woods. The monsters did not see me. Hidden by the trees, I pushed on toward home.

If I had been thinking clearly, I would have gone back to Leather-head. To my wife. But I was wet, tired, and blinded by the storm. All I could think of was home.

But I still had a hill to climb. That was the hardest task of all in the storm.

Near the top, I stepped on something soft. A flash of lightning showed me a pair of boots. It was a man!

I turned him over. He was quite dead. A second lightning flash showed me his face. It was the landlord of the Spotted Dog Inn! He would never again need the horse and cart I had used. I felt sad, but I kept going.

At last I saw my own house. Once inside, I quickly locked the door. I felt safer now.

I sat down on the stairs. My head was full of huge metal monsters. And the dead face of the landlord of the Spotted Dog. I shook all over.

Chapter 6

At last I went to my room and put on dry clothes. I drank a little whiskey and sat by the window. The tall college towers were gone. Now I could see the area around the pit. It was lit by a strange red glare. Huge dark shapes moved to and fro. They looked very busy.

The whole countryside nearby seemed to be on fire. Flames were everywhere. A sharp smell of burning was in the air.

Yellow boxes were lying near the railroad tracks. What could they be? Then I knew. A wrecked train!

I watched those busy shapes near the pit. Were they Martians? Were they machines? Was a Martian inside each one?

Then I thought of human machines. How would they seem to a smart monkey? All this was not so different. Only we humans were the "monkeys" this time.

I heard a scraping sound and saw a soldier in my garden.

"Hist," said I, in a whisper.

"Who is there?" he whispered back.

"Where are you going?" I asked.

"Trying to hide," he said.

"Come into the house."

I let him in. Then I locked the door again.

"What has happened?" I asked.

"They wiped us out," he said. "Just wiped us out."

"Sit down," I said.

He did. Then his head went down on the table. He began to sob like a little boy.

I let him cry it out. When he stopped, he told me his story.

He had been with a large group of soldiers, shooting at some Martians. During the battle, the soldier's horse tripped and fell on him. He fell into a hole. At that same moment, the heat-ray hit everyone around him. He was the only soldier left alive. The hole had saved him.

"I had hurt my back," he said. "I lay still a long time. Scared out of my wits. And with the front part of the horse on top of me. At last I got up. Then I saw that not a man or a horse was left standing. Every bush and tree around was burning. It was horrible.

"Later," he went on, "the heat-ray got the town, too."

"Did you see any other people?" I asked him.

"Yes," he said. "I saw a few. Burned. Hurt. In a panic."

The poor soldier had not eaten all day. I found some food. We ate in darkness. We were afraid that the Martians would see a light.

Chapter 7

Dawn came. Three giant Martian machines were still working in the pit. Now and then, a puff of green smoke rose into the air.

The fires had become a dull glow. Destruction was everywhere.

We agreed that the house was not a safe place to stay. The soldier would head to London to find his regiment. I would go to Leatherhead.

The soldier knew we should take along food. We stuffed our pockets. Then we crept out of the house.

Everything that was not dead or blackened was burning. Here and there things people had dropped. A clock. A slipper. A silver spoon.

At last we met an officer and two soldiers. They were riding to the pit to fight. "What's going on?" the officer asked.

"Our big gun was destroyed last night, sir," said my soldier friend. "And all our men and horses except me. I'm trying to find my regiment now. You will see the Martians about half a mile down this road."

"What are they like?" the officer asked.

"Giants, sir. Monsters," said my friend. "A hundred feet high. Three legs and a metal body."

"Get out!" said the officer. "You must be kidding."

"You'll see, sir. They carry a box. It shoots fire that kills." My friend described the heat-ray.

"It's true," I said.

The officer didn't know what to think. That was clear.

"We'll see for ourselves," he said. He thanked us, and we parted.

Soon my friend and I were in the town of Byfleet. It was far from the heat-ray. People were slowly packing to go. Carts and wagons were everywhere. One man was packing a dozen pots of flowers! Soldiers were trying to make the people hurry.

Six large cannons were pointed toward Woking. There was a pile of shells nearby. Farther on we saw soldiers putting up a wall. And more cannons.

"Bows and arrows against lightning," said my friend. "They haven't seen the heat-ray yet."

We went on to a town where two rivers met. There was a crowd of excited people carrying all sorts of goods. They were all trying to rent boats to cross the river. A big ferryboat was packed with people.

"What's that?" cried a boatman.

We heard the thud, thud of guns. The sound grew louder. The fighting was all around us. But trees hid the guns from sight.

Suddenly we saw a rush of smoke.

We heard a shattering blast. Then one, two, three, four of the metal Martians appeared! One held the terrible heat-ray machine.

People saw the monsters. They were struck silent with horror. Then they started to rush into the water.

I turned and ran to the beach. Get under water. That was it! People from the boats splashed into the river all around me.

I raised my head to breathe. That is when I saw the Martian with the heat-ray. It was walking across the water on its long legs. The monster was about to shoot its heat-ray at the town. Would it hit the soldiers? No! *They* hit the monster's head.

The Martian inside it must have been killed. But the headless machine kept walking like a drunken monster. It crashed into houses. It smashed down the church tower. The heat-ray was locked in one of its tentacles. Then it fell into the water with great force.

And *boom!* It blew up. Water, steam, and metal flew into the sky.

A yell of terror made me turn. Four other Martians were coming!

The guns fired at them. But this time there was no hit.

I ducked under water at once. I stayed under as long as I could. But I had to breathe. And the water was getting very hot.

When I came up, I saw the other four monsters standing in the water. They were bent over the "dead" Martian machine.

They care about each other, I
thought. I was amazed. And wrong!
What they wanted was the heat-ray.
And they got it. They fired it back
and forth. Houses, trees, and sheds
crashed and burst into flames.

Just then the white flashes of the
heat-ray turned toward me. The
Martians fired it all around me. It
licked up the people running out of
the water.

Once again I was not hit. But the

water was boiling. Screaming in pain and almost blind, I headed for the shore. The hissing water leaped around me.

A huge wave nearly knocked me over. But at last I reached the shore. Too tired to move. In full sight of the Martians, I waited for death.

One of them was only a few feet away. But they paid no attention to me. Instead, the four Martian machines carried off the "dead" one. I was still alive. Very slowly I realized I had escaped.

Chapter 8

If they pushed on, the Martians could wipe out our whole country. Then and there. Our guns had killed only one of them. We were no match for the Martians and their monster machines. But they were in no hurry.

Day after day other cylinders landed. Each one carried more Martians and more machines. The first pit seemed to be their planning center.

The army worked hard to control them. Big cannons and fresh soldiers kept arriving. They took up positions in a twenty-mile circle. They stayed hidden. They now knew the dangers of going too near the cylinders. No one went closer than a mile, except a few brave scouts. The scouts sent signals to the soldiers.

The Martians spent the next day working. They put everything from the second and third cylinder into their pit. They were planning their next move.

I headed for London. I was lucky enough to find an empty boat. Water was my best chance to escape the monsters. I paddled with my burned hands.

After a while, I had to stop. I felt tired and sick. I lay down in the grass and slept.

Then I opened my eyes. I saw a dirty man sitting near me.

"Have you any water?" I asked. I felt very thirsty.

He shook his head. "You have been asking for water for an hour," he said.

Then we stared at each other. We each made a strange sight. His light blue eyes had an empty look.

"What does it mean?" he asked. "Are these monsters everywhere? What are we to do?"

He was very upset.

"You must keep your head," said I. "There is still hope."

I tried to explain my plans. But he could not listen long. His mind was far away.

"How can we escape the Martians and their machines?" he asked at last. "They are too big and too strong."

"The stronger they are, the more calm we must be," I answered.

From far away came the sound of guns.

"Listen!" he said.

"We had better get away from here," I said.

Henry followed me north. Henry was my new friend.

Soon we saw two of the huge metal Martians. They held heat-rays. Henry ran in a panic. I knew running would not help. So I crawled into a ditch to hide. Henry saw me and did the same.

All was still. We waited for the shooting to start. But it didn't. We could see the huge machines walking away from us.

We did not know what was happening around us. We did not know that another cylinder had landed. We did not know that London was in danger now. So we kept on going north toward London.

Chapter 9

Henry and I talked very little. I kept thinking about my wife. Was she safe? Did she think I was dead? I made up my mind to head toward Leatherhead.

Things had gotten quiet. We started to feel almost safe. Then we saw some people running. A moment later, we saw a Martian machine very close to us. High above some houses. We hid in the first place we could find. A shed in a garden.

Henry sat down and cried. He would not move. But I was in a rush to get to Leatherhead. I *had* to find my wife. So I left Henry in the shed.

I started on my way again. Henry came hurrying after me.

Both of us should have stayed in the shed. As soon as we left, we saw that Martian machine again. It was picking up people one by one. Putting them into a metal bag. The way we might pick fruit or flowers.

At first Henry and I just stood there. Too horrified to move. Now the Martians were taking people alive! What would they do to them?

We hid in a ditch until dark. In darkness we could sneak out safely.

When had we last eaten? We broke into an empty house. There was no food in it. But we found water to drink.

The next house we tried had a lot to eat. Bread, meat, beans, and soup. Lucky for us. We were trapped in that house for two weeks.

After we had eaten a good meal, we felt better. All at once, there was a glare of bright green light. Then a thud and the crash of glass. Plaster fell from the ceiling. It knocked me out for a while.

Henry helped me sit up. I could see that the room was still dark.

"Don't move," he whispered. "There is glass all over the floor. If you move, you will make noise. And I think *they* are out there!"

We sat in silence. We heard the sound of metal rattling outside.

"A Martian!" Henry said.

We sat still all night. Wondering what was going on. In the morning we saw. Most of the house had caved in!

I looked through a crack. A Martian machine was standing outside. Next to it was a spaceship.

"Another cylinder!" I whispered. "It landed right on this house. And it buried us inside."

"God have mercy on us!" whispered Henry. He started to cry again.

There was no sound but his sobs. I stayed as still as can be. Then came hammering from outside. Then hooting. Then hissing. What could be making these noises? We did not know.

I must have fallen asleep. It was dawn when I awoke. Henry sat with his eye next to the hole. I crept over and touched his arm. He jumped. A mass of plaster fell with a loud crash. Would the Martians hear? The two of us hid.

But the plaster had left a bigger crack. Now both of us could see outside at the same time.

I saw the cylinder. It had made a big pit when it landed. Just as the first spaceship had. Its landing had smashed many houses. Most of this house was smashed as well. But somehow the rooms we were in had been saved.

A large Martian machine was digging. It was making the pit bigger. It made the hissing noises.

The machine looked like a huge spider. It had five legs and many tentacles. It used the tentacles to do its work.

It moved quickly and perfectly. At first I thought it was alive. But it was metal. It had to be a machine.

More amazing were the strange creatures near it. They were crawling around very slowly. As if moving hurt them. They were the real Martians.

They were nothing but huge round

heads. No bodies. Each had a face in front. On it were two eyes and a beak. No nose. Around the beak were sixteen thin tentacles. The back of the head was one big ear.

The Martians had no legs. They tried to get up on their tentacles. But on Earth they were too heavy to do it.

I know now what was inside each huge Martian's head. A brain, lungs, and a heart. That's all. They had no stomachs. They did not eat the way we do. So they didn't need stomachs. They were heads. Just heads.

How did they live? What they did was not pretty. I saw them do it. They took blood from live animals. Mostly humans. They injected it into themselves. Seeing this made me sick. But I will tell you more when I get to that.

There are probably no green plants on Mars. The Martians had brought seeds with them. Bright red weeds grew from these seeds. They grew *very* big.

In the pit, I saw the red weed start out small. It covered all the sides of the pit after only four days. Later I saw the same plants everywhere I went. Wherever there was water, anyway.

We were trapped inside the house. A door led outside. But it opened only a little. Anyway, we could not leave without being seen. The Martians were everywhere. They didn't need to sleep. So we had no chance to sneak away.

All Henry and I could do was watch the Martians closely. I probably saw more of them than any other person did. Sometimes they "talked" without sound. That is, they read each other's minds. At other times they made howls like sirens. Up and down the scale from note to note.

The Martians had no bodies for clothes. What they wore were their machines. I mean that a Martian was inside each machine. They controlled the machines. The way a human runs a bicycle or a car.

These Martians were almost all brain. So they made machines to do the things they could not do.

Chapter 10

Getting along with Henry became harder and harder. I could not stand him. He acted like a spoiled child. He ate too much. I warned him that we would soon run out of food. But he kept doing it.

I would get very angry. I even hit Henry. He cried and hit me back.

More huge Martian machines arrived. We saw them from our crack in the wall. We felt terribly scared. But we still peeped through the hole from time to time.

The machines moved quickly. The real Martians moved slowly. Could these slow creatures really be the live ones? I had to wonder.

One day I heard human voices. I looked outside but saw no one. Then I saw a machine grab something from a cage. It was a man! The machine took him away. I heard him scream. What would happen to him?

I found out soon enough. The Martians were using a thin pipe to take blood from the live man. Then they piped his blood into themselves. They kept on until all his blood was gone. Would the Martians use me that way too? I knew Henry and I had to escape.

I tried to dig a way out for us. But digging made too much noise. I had to stop. If only we could get out the door. But the Martians would see us.

Henry was no help. The next day I found him drinking wine. I grabbed it from him. Then I divided all the food into ten parts. That way it would last us ten days.

I would not let Henry eat any more that day. He kept trying to steal more. He cried like a child. He was hungry. But I kept him from the food.

I tried everything with Henry. I threatened. I talked sweetly to him. I even bribed him with the last bit of wine. But he kept stealing food. And he kept crying. I knew he had lost his mind.

Then he began to talk loudly. I begged him to stop. He threatened to yell. That would bring a Martian on us.

That terrified me. But he did not yell. He just kept talking loud and crying.

"Be still!" I begged.

"I have been still too long," Henry shouted.

"Shut up!" I whispered.

"No," he said. "I must go."

I tried to grab him. But he slipped through the small opening in the door. He walked straight up to a Martian machine. The machine grabbed him. I could not watch anymore. I turned away.

Just then I saw a tentacle. It was coming through the crack in the wall.

Then came another. I kept still. Too terrified to move.

At last I crawled to the cellar. Had the Martian seen me? What was it doing now?

I could hear it moving. Very, very slowly. But I stayed put. Hiding in a coal bin.

I listened. I heard the Martian moving around. At last it was at the cellar door. I heard the lock. Then the door opened. The Martians understood doors!

I dared not breathe. The Martian moved slowly about the cellar. I could see a tentacle touching things. It looked like an elephant's trunk.

Once it touched the heel of my boot. I almost screamed. I bit my hand instead.

Click! The Martian grabbed something. I thought it had me! But I think it took a lump of coal.

The Martian seemed to go out of the cellar again. I heard it shut the door. Then all was quiet.

Had it gone?

At last I decided that it had. But I

did not dare move. I hid in the cellar all that day. I did not even go out for a drink of water.

I stayed right where I was until the next day. Hunger finally forced me to leave the cellar. But every scrap of food was gone. The Martians must have taken it. I don't know why. Martians don't eat food.

I was so thirsty I tried the rain-water pump. I drank the dirty water.

For the next two days I ate nothing. I fell asleep and woke. My dreams were of food. Or Henry's death. I felt hopeless.

No sounds came from the pit. Had I become deaf? I was too weak to look out the peephole.

Three more days passed without a sound from the Martians. Some of their red weed was growing through the peephole. I overcame my fear and pushed it aside and looked.

There was nothing in the pit but red weeds! No Martians. No machines. My chance for escape had come.

I squeezed through the door. All around were skeletons and a few crows. Smashed houses and the red weeds. That was all.

I climbed out of the pit. Away from the place that had been my prison. And, oh, the fresh air seemed so sweet!

Chapter 11

First I needed food. I saw a green patch of garden. No red weed grew over it. But to reach it, I had to walk through the red weed. In places it reached to my neck.

Then I had to climb a wall. But the trip was worth it. I found onions and carrots!

I was ready to start on my way. As I walked I found mushrooms and water. Not much for a very hungry man.

Wherever there was water, the red weed grew. I tried to eat some. But it tasted terrible.

I walked all that day. I saw no human beings. And no Martians. Only two hungry-looking dogs. Nothing else living. Was the human race gone forever? Was I the last man on Earth?

That night I slept in a real bed in an empty inn. First I looked for food. I found an old sandwich, too rotten to eat. But two cans of pineapple were good.

I lay awake worrying most of the night. Where were the Martians? Would they find me? Was my wife alive? I did not have a hint about any of it.

The morning was sunny. I started on my way again. Where to? Maybe Leatherhead. My wife would have run from there. But I might learn where she had gone.

I walked and walked, feeling lonely. Then I saw a man holding a dagger! He looked as dirty as I did.

His face was cut. Black hair fell over his eyes.

"Stop!" he cried. "Where do you come from?"

I told him my story.

"There is no food here," he said. "This is my country. There is only food for one."

"I'm on my way to Leatherhead. Don't worry," I said.

"It's you!" he said, and smiled. "The man from Woking."

"And you are the soldier who came into my garden!" I cried.

"We are the lucky ones," he said.

We shook hands. He invited me to a proper meal. He was living in a big house on a hill. It was stocked with good food and wine. We even smoked cigars and played cards. Strange as that may seem.

Perhaps we both needed to escape from the horror of our lives. But of course the horror returned.

"Have you seen any Martians?" I asked.

"They have gone away to London," he said. "Been gone for five days now. Last I saw them with a flying machine. They are learning to fly."

"Fly!" I cried.

"Yes, fly," he said.

"Then they will fly around the world," said I. "Killing and burning. The human race is done for."

"We are beat," the soldier agreed. "It's all over. They have not begun on us yet. These Martians are getting things ready. Then the rest of their kind will come."

"Yes," I said. "I'm afraid you're right."

"We are the ones who have escaped," said the soldier. "We must get ready."

"What can we do?" I asked.

"We must hide for now. Underground. In railroad tunnels. Drains. Cellars," said he. "And we must form a band. Only strong men and women. No weak or lazy ones allowed."

He went on.

"We must make safe places deep underground. Get all the science books we can. Learn more. Watch the Martians. Spy on them. But we must leave them alone. We must show them we mean no harm. They will forget about us."

The soldier took my arm.

"We will learn all that the Martians know," he said. "Then one day people will be inside the machines. Not Martians. We will have the heat-ray. And the human race will come back to its own!"

That all sounded good. But it would never happen. I knew this soldier was a dreamer. I would go on to London and learn what was happening.

Chapter 12

After I left the soldier, I went into London. Most of the city looked like it did on a Sunday. The shops were closed. The houses were locked up. The streets were still.

When I got deep into London, I heard sad howling. "Ulla, ulla, ulla." The sound of the first Martian. "Ulla, ulla, ulla."

I heard it down every street. It came out from between the tall buildings. It did not stop.

Soon it got to be too much for me. I felt tired and hungry. I was very lonely.

I broke into an empty inn. I found

food and wine. Then I slept on a couch.

I awoke to the sound of the same howling. "Ulla, ulla, ulla."

I left the inn and walked to a park. There I saw a huge Martian machine. It was turned on its side. Not moving. Its tentacles were bent and twisted. The howling came from inside the giant. "Ulla, ulla, ulla."

No longer did the machine frighten me. So I did not hide. I kept going.

I passed the zoo. There I saw another huge Martian machine. It too was standing still. But it made not a sound.

Here and there I saw the red weed. It was starting to turn brown.

All at once, the sad howling

stopped. The air was silent. Now I felt frightened. London was a ghost city. And I was alone in it.

Then I saw yet another Martian machine. And as I got nearer, I saw birds flying around its head. I knew what this meant. I began to run toward the monster.

Yes! The birds were picking at a dead Martian inside the machine.

I looked around me. I was standing in one of the Martian pits. I saw more machines lying on the ground. At least fifty. Around them were the real Martians. All were dead!

The machines glittered in the morning sunshine. Harmless giants.

I did not learn until later what had killed the Martians. Earth's germs! Bacteria. Germs were killing the red

weed as well. There are no germs on Mars. So Martians cannot fight germs as our bodies can. The howling I heard was the Martians as they were dying.

It was all over. The human race was saved. I began weeping and thanking God.

I thought then of my wife. Maybe we would be together again after all! Maybe life would go on.

Chapter 13

Now comes the strangest thing in my story. I remember nothing of the next three days.

Later I learned that I was not the only man to see the Martians dying. Others had sent out the word the night before.

Church bells were ringing all over England. The whole world was full of joy. Food and help were on the way from many countries. But I was in a daze. Wandering. Weeping.

One day I found myself in a house. Some kind people had taken care of me. When I was well again, these people told me about Leatherhead.

It had been burned by the heat-ray. Nothing of the town or its people was left.

I was a sad, lonely man. I wanted to go to my old home. Even if I would have no wife there. So I kissed my new friends good-bye.

London was coming back to life. People were coming home. Some looked happy. Some looked grim. Every other person was wearing rags. The French had sent bread. The churches were handing it out. Some shops were even open.

Free trains were taking people to their homes. So I got on one. I sat alone with folded arms. Ruined fields and villages flowed past the window. I got off at Woking and walked to my house.

I went in feeling some hope. But the house was empty. Curtains flapped at the open window. The soldier and I had left the window open. No one had shut it. I looked around. All was as I had left it. But now it felt sad and lonely.

Then I heard a voice I knew.

"It's no use," it said. "The house is empty. No one has been here."

I was startled. I turned and looked out the open window.

And there were my wife and her cousin.

"I came," cried my wife. "I knew. I knew. . . ."

Chapter 14

I wish I could teach my readers more about the Martians. But I am not an expert.

Will the Martians ever come back? No one knows. But we should be ready. Just in case. Then we could destroy any spaceship that landed. Right away.

But some scientists have another idea. They think the Martians have landed on the planet Venus. They have seen lights moving from Mars to Venus. The scientists may be right. Who knows?

We have learned a lot from what happened here. First, we used to

think only Earth had life. Now we
know better. Second, if the Martians
can reach Venus, why can't we?

I have a picture in my mind. A
wonderful picture. I see the people
of Earth spreading through space.
They are landing on Venus. Mars.
The moon! But of course that is just
a dream.

H. G. Wells was born in England in 1866 and studied biology and history. He wrote serious books on both subjects. But he is best known for such science-fiction adventures as *The Time Machine* and *The War of the Worlds.* He wrote about submarines, flight, and space travel before there were even automobiles!

Mary Ann Evans is a freelance photographer and editor. She lives in Carmel, New York. She enjoys taking long hikes with her golden retrievers.

Paul Wenzel has been an artist with the Walt Disney Company for almost thirty years. He has illustrated a number of children's books. He is also a gallery artist, best known for his paintings of Native Americans.